NIGHT OF THE WEREPOODLE

Weekly Reader Book Club Presents

NIGHT OF THE WEREPOODLE

Constance Hiser

drawings by Cynthia Fisher

Holiday House/New York

This book is a presentation of Newfield Publications, Inc.
Newfield Publications offers book clubs for children from
preschool through high school. For further information
write to: **Newfield Publications, Inc.,** 4343 Equity Drive,
Columbus, Ohio 43228.

Published by arrangement with Holiday House.
Newfield Publications is a federally registered
trademark of Newfield Publications, Inc.
Weekly Reader is a federally registered trademark
of Weekly Reader Corporation.

Library of Congress Cataloging-in-Publication Data
Hiser, Constance.
Night of the werepoodle / Constance Hiser; drawings by
Cynthia Fisher. — 1st ed.
p.   cm.
Summary: Having been turned into a werepoodle by the bite
of his neighbor's dog, Jonathan must find a missing wolfbane
chewbone or be doomed to remain a beast forever.
ISBN 0-8234-1116-8
[1. Supernatural—Fiction. 2. Dogs—Fiction.] I. Fisher,
Cynthia, ill. II. Title.
PZ7.H618Ni   1994   93-25732   CIP
[Fic]—dc20

Contents

CHAPTER ONE

A Vampire
in Fourth Grade

I can't believe it, Jonathan thought, straightening his glasses with a shaky hand. Just when I was starting to think everything was going to be okay, changing schools and all. Just when I was starting to learn my way around. Just when—

"Well, Four-Eyes?" Vince clenched a big fist and shook it right under Jonathan's nose. His rust-colored hair bristled wildly around his scowling, freckle-splotched face. "Are you blind *and* deaf? I said, I

1

want your lunch money, and I want it *right now.*"

"Come on, Vince, give me a break." Jonathan tried to sound brave, which wasn't easy when the bully had just clutched the front of his sweatshirt and slammed his back against the brick wall of the school building. "You have lunch money of your own, don't you? You don't need mine. Besides, if you take my money, what will I have for lunch?"

"Ooooh!" Vince pretended to be horrified. "Why didn't *I* think of that? How can I possibly enjoy spending your lunch money, if I have to think about you going hungry all day? Oh, please do forgive me, then shut your mouth and hand over the cash!"

"But, Vince—" Jonathan began.

"Boy, you *are* dumb, aren't you, Four-Eyes?" Vince growled, shoving his fist even closer. "I'm going to tell you one more time. Give me your lunch money, or else!"

"Okay, okay," Jonathan agreed, hastily

pulling the dollar and two quarters from his jeans pocket. "Now will you please let me go, so we won't both be late for school?"

"Oh dear, we wouldn't want to be late, would we?" Vince said, laughing. "Not two good little boys like us. Well, thanks for the money, Four-Eyes. See you around."

He gave Jonathan's shoulders a last shake, letting go so suddenly that Jonathan almost fell. Then, whistling under his breath, Vince ambled around the corner of the school building and disappeared.

"Wow, that was a close one!" Tony Scarlatti ran over from the jungle gym the minute Vince was out of sight. Tony was followed by Roger and Patrick, and a second later Missy, Jennifer, and Alyssa arrived, out of breath from running all the way from the swings.

"We saw what happened," Alyssa gasped, so excited she could hardly get the words out. "We thought he was going to hit you for sure."

4

"Yeah." Roger shook his head. "And when Vince the Vampire hits you, believe me, you feel it."

"Vampire?" Jonathan echoed shakily, smoothing the creases from his sweatshirt. "What do you mean, Vince the Vampire? He just grabbed me. He didn't bite me—yet."

"We've called him that ever since first grade," Jennifer explained. "Ever since he socked Tommy Mellandorf in the nose and Tommy bled all over the boys' room floor. Tommy said he hadn't seen so much blood since the last vampire movie he'd watched. So we just started saying 'Vince the Vampire.' It fits him pretty well."

"Yeah," Jonathan agreed, picking up the books and papers he had dropped on the ground when Vince grabbed him. School hadn't even started yet, and already Jonathan felt tired. "I see what you mean. There was a guy like that at my old school, too, but I think Vince is even worse."

"He's the worst bully ever," Patrick said.

He sounded almost proud. "Everyone's scared of Vince the Vampire."

"So why don't you do something about him?" Jonathan demanded. "If he's been picking on people since first grade, why do you let him get away with it?"

"What do you mean?" Missy asked with a puzzled frown. "What could we do about it? Vince is bigger and stronger than everyone in fourth grade. And he's just smart enough not to bother anyone when a teacher is watching. So he never gets sent to the office or anything. How could we stop him?"

"I don't know," Jonathan admitted. "We never did figure out a way to stop the bully at my old school either. But I sure hate losing my lunch money. It's a long time till supper."

"That's okay," Tony said. "You can share part of my lunch. I brought mine today, and my mom always sends two sandwiches."

"And you can have some of my cookies for dessert," Alyssa offered.

"We'll all share," Roger promised. "Sit with us at lunch, okay? That way you won't have to go hungry."

Jonathan grinned for the first time that morning.

"Thanks, guys," he said. "That's terrific."

"There goes the bell," Jennifer squealed. "We'd better hurry or we'll be late."

They sprinted around the corner toward the front door of the school, where kids were already lining up to go inside.

Jonathan followed slowly, his breath making little puffs of fog in the chilly November air. His morning had gotten off to a lousy start, but maybe things weren't going to be so bad after all. At least today he'd have some new friends to sit with at lunch.

That made it worth losing his lunch money.

CHAPTER TWO

Wish I Were a Werewolf

Tony's mom made good ham sandwiches, and the cookies and fruit the other kids shared were fine, too. But the cafeteria was serving gooey, sloppy, delicious-looking pepperoni-and-cheese pizza, and Jonathan's mouth watered every time he looked at it. If Vince the Vampire hadn't stolen his lunch money, he could have had pizza for lunch.

By the time the last bell rang at three-thirty, Jonathan was so hungry his stomach was growling. As he waved good-bye to his new friends at the corner of the playground, all he could think about was getting home to a nice, thick peanut-butter-and-jelly sandwich and a big glass of cold chocolate milk. This was Mom's night to work late, so dinner wouldn't be for hours yet. Jonathan just hoped she had remembered to buy a new jar of peanut butter.

He was trying to decide between strawberry jam and grape jelly on his sandwich when he rounded the corner of Apple Street and passed by the little redbrick house where old Mr. Bruce, his next-door neighbor, lived. Maybe he would have *two* sandwiches, he thought, fumbling in his jeans pocket for his house key, one with grape jelly and one with strawberry jam. And as long as he was at it, he might as well have a piece of that chocolate cake Mom had brought home last night. And after that—

"Rrrrrufff! Row, row, row, ruff!"

Jonathan spun around to see a little

white poodle yapping excitedly at his feet. Oh, great, he thought. Just what I need—teeth marks all over my new running shoes.

"Scat!" he yelled, waving his arms to shoo the dog away. "Go away, dog, you hear? Leave me alone!"

"Ruff!" the poodle yipped. "Rrr, rrr, rrr, ruff!" It seemed to be trying hard to look tough as it darted forward again and again to snap at Jonathan's shoes.

"What do you think you are, a Dober-man?" Jonathan snorted. "You aren't scaring me, dog, but I don't have time for this. Beat it!"

"Charlemagne!"

A stern voice made Jonathan's head snap up. Old Mr. Bruce was hurrying down the front walk, shaking his finger at the little poodle. Mr. Bruce's thick, flowing beard streamed as white as snow down the front of his black sweater, and his long white hair floated past his shoulders. His silver-gray eyes flashed as he scolded his pet.

"Charlemagne, you bad dog! How many times have I told you not to bother people? You get back inside this fence this minute!"

The little dog's yapping stopped as suddenly as if someone had pushed the Off switch on a tape recorder. Glancing sheepishly at Jonathan, the poodle scuttled through the open gate and hid behind his master's ankles.

"I'm sorry about that," the old man apologized, leaning over the fence to shake Jonathan's hand. A huge, bloodred stone glittered from the ring on his gnarled finger. "Charlie digs holes under this fence faster than I can patch them up. And then he has to bark at everyone who walks by. He wouldn't really have bitten you, though. Charlie's all talk, aren't you, boy?"

The little dog wagged its tail, seeming to laugh.

"That's okay," Jonathan said. "I like dogs. I used to have one, but he died when I was six."

"Well, you're welcome to play with Charlemagne anytime," Mr. Bruce promised. "Your name is Jonathan, isn't it? I heard your mother calling you in for supper the other night."

"That's right," Jonathan answered. "And I already know your name is Mr. Bruce. It says so on your mailbox."

"Smart kid," his neighbor chuckled. "Well, Jonathan, I guess I'll be taking this bad dog of mine inside now. He doesn't know it yet, but it's time for his b-a-t-h."

"Good luck!" Jonathan laughed, as the old man headed back up the walk with the poodle following at his heels. He sure was glad he didn't have to give that yappy little dog a bath!

Jonathan unlocked his front door, quickly hung up his coat, put his books on the dining room table, and headed for the kitchen to fix himself a snack. Mom had left him a note, stuck to the refrigerator with a little flower-shaped magnet. Jonathan took it down and read it as he got out the milk.

"Dear Jonathan," Mom had written, "the office won't be closing till seven tonight. There's a meat loaf mixed and ready in the refrigerator. Would you please put it in the oven at 350° around six? And it would help if you'd set the table, too. See you around seven. Love, Mom."

Well, that settled it. If supper were going to be *that* late, he was definitely going to have a piece of chocolate cake. Maybe two.

He found the peanut butter in the cabinet, then checked the breadbox for bread. He had plenty of time for a snack. And come to think of it, Mrs. Young hadn't given much homework tonight. Maybe he even had time to watch the late-afternoon monster movie on Channel 32 while he ate. He could always do his spelling after supper.

14

Jonathan bit nervously into his sandwich, not even noticing when the grape jelly oozed from the sides and spattered down the front of his sweatshirt. The monster movie was scarier than most of the movies on Channel 32, and Jonathan was glad he wasn't watching it late at night. *The Deadly Claw of the Werewolf* was spooky enough in broad daylight.

"Wow," he whispered to himself, as the werewolf growled, showing what looked like a hundred sharp, white teeth. "I wish that guy had been there when Vince the Vampire grabbed me this morning."

As a matter of fact, he thought, it would be even better if *he* could be a werewolf. Not forever, of course, like the poor guy in the movie. Just for a little while. Just long enough to teach Vince a lesson he'd never forget. First, he'd grab Vince with his long, needle-sharp claws and see how *he* liked having *his* good clothes all messed up. Then he'd open his mouth, and when Vince saw all those teeth . . .

15

"Bong!" Jonathan jumped as the clock in the dining room began to strike. Six o'clock already! He'd better get that meat loaf in the oven, or Mom would have a fit. There was a commercial coming on, anyway.

"You don't get it, do you, Four-Eyes?" Vince sighed impatiently, giving Jonathan a little shake. "When I tell you I want your lunch money, I don't mean whenever you get around to it. I mean *right now!* And I don't want a lot of your lip either!"

"But, Vince—" Jonathan began desperately. He didn't want to miss lunch two days in a row.

"But nothing!" Vince growled. "If I don't see that money by the time I count to three, I'm going to be in a very bad mood. And you don't want that to happen, do you, wimp? Now give it here! One, two—"

"Okay, okay!" Fishing the money from his pocket, Jonathan thrust it into the bully's hand. "Now let me go, okay? I have to go to the rest room."

"Yeah." Vince grinned his nasty grin. "Wouldn't want you to have an accident, would we, Four-Eyes? See you tomorrow, baby!"

When Vince had gone, Jonathan slumped weakly against the school wall. Was Vince the Vampire going to take his lunch money every single day? At this rate, he could starve to death by Christmas break.

"Boy," he muttered under his breath, "I really *do* wish I were a werewolf. Then he'd never dare mess with me again."

But there didn't seem to be much chance of that. So Jonathan sighed, collected his scattered books, and headed into the building.

It looked as if it were going to be another long, long day.

CHAPTER THREE

Little Dog, Big Teeth

"I still don't understand why you suddenly want me to pack your lunch," Jonathan's mom said the next morning as she reached for the sandwich bags. "I thought you said the school cafeteria served great lunches."

"They do," Jonathan answered, gulping the last of his orange juice. "I just wanted to do something different today. Thanks, Mom. Oh, and Mom, could I have a couple of those cupcakes you bought? I'll be really hungry by lunchtime."

"Help yourself," his mother answered. "I have to hurry or I'll be late for work. Make sure you lock the front door when you leave, okay?"

Five minutes later, Jonathan shut and locked the door behind him. His jacket was zipped against the frosty autumn breeze. His bookbag thumped against his back, and he carried the brown paper sack with his lunch in it.

This is one morning ol' Vince the Vampire won't get *my* lunch money, he told himself, as he marched down the front walk. In fact, that creep's never going to get another penny from me, even if I have to take my lunch every day for the rest of the school year.

Jonathan was feeling so good about outwitting the class bully that he didn't hear the footsteps behind him on the sidewalk. He didn't know anyone was near until he suddenly felt himself being grabbed by the back of his jacket and slammed against Mr. Bruce's fence. He gasped for air as he

19

gazed up into the grinning face of Vince the Vampire.

"Oh, no!" Jonathan groaned when he could speak again. "What are you doing here? What do you want this time?"

"What do you think I want, twerp?" the bully chuckled. "Come on, I don't have all day. Hand it over."

"Hand over what?" Jonathan asked, feeling his heart dive into his shoes.

"Your lunch money, what else?" Vince sounded impatient. "I'm not in the mood for games, Four-Eyes. Now, are you going to give me that money, or do I have to get rough?"

"But—but I don't even have any lunch money today!" Jonathan argued. "My mother packed my lunch, see?" And he held up his lunch bag.

Vince's eyes narrowed angrily. "What are you trying to pull?" he demanded. "This isn't just some trick to keep me from getting your money, is it?"

Jonathan shook his head quickly back

and forth. "Of course not," he said desperately. "Would I do that to you, Vince? My—my mother didn't have any money in the house for my lunch today, so she packed it instead. That's it, I promise." He hoped Vince wouldn't see that he had the fingers of one hand crossed behind his back.

"Hmmm." Vince stared at the brown paper bag. "Well, as long as your mother went to all the trouble of packing you such a yummy lunch, I guess the least I can do is check it out, right? I know your mom would want you to share with your good ol' buddy Vince, wouldn't she? I said, *wouldn't she?*"

"Please, Vince, give me a break!" Jonathan begged, but Vince had already grabbed the lunch bag and ripped it open.

"Why, Jonathan, I'm really disappointed in your mom," the bully said. "I thought she'd make you better lunches than this. Why, there's no way I can let a friend of mine eat a disgusting lunch like this. No way! Which means there's just one thing for me to do."

And before Jonathan knew what was about to happen, Vince had dropped his lunch in the middle of the sidewalk and stomped on it—hard. As he ground his foot through the brown paper bag, tuna salad oozed from the sandwiches and chocolate squirted from the cupcakes to blend with the yellow bits of crushed potato chips.

"My lunch!" Jonathan yelped. Suddenly he was so angry that he forgot to be afraid. "I ought to punch you for that!" he shouted. "I ought to pound your face in, you big jerk! I ought to—"

"Yeah?" Suddenly Vince the Vampire wasn't grinning anymore. "What were you saying, Four-Eyes? What are you gonna do to me, huh?"

Jonathan ignored the little voice inside his head that told him he was about to get his brains mashed to a pulp.

"You're a big bully, and that's all you are, Vince!" he yelled, standing on tiptoe and glaring into the other boy's furious face. "Someday the rest of us will grow, and then you won't be the biggest kid in the class anymore. And when that happens, you'd just better look out. Because—"

"Ruff! Ruff! Row, row, row, ruff!"

Both boys jumped as a small whirlwind of white fur exploded through a hole under the fence. Charlie rushed down the sidewalk toward them, running so fast that he was only a blur.

"Back, Charlie!" Jonathan yelled. "Get back, you dumb dog! He'll kill you!"

Now Vince was smiling again. "I will, too," he said. "Wimpy little dust mop. Where's he get off, calling himself a dog?"

Frantically, Jonathan threw himself between Vince and the furiously charging poodle, just as Vince aimed a kick at the little dog's head.

"Ouch!" Jonathan screamed as two things happened at once. Vince's kick connected with Jonathan's leg, and Charlie's

sharp little teeth sank into Jonathan's ankle.

"That's what you get for trying to be a hero," Vince laughed as he aimed another kick at the dog.

"Hey, what's going on here?"

Jonathan went limp with relief as Mr. Bruce hobbled down the front walk, glaring at Vince.

"Hey, you—the big boy. What are you doing to my dog?" the old man demanded, his beard bristling with anger. "And look, you've hurt Jonathan. I think I'll call the police!"

"Oh, yeah?" Vince snarled. "Well, you'll have to catch me first, won't you?"

And he pelted off down the street, quickly disappearing around the corner onto Zinnia Street.

"Are you all right?" Mr. Bruce asked, helping Jonathan to his feet. "I saw what happened, but I couldn't move fast enough to get here in time. You probably saved Charlie's life, you know. I think that boy really would have hurt him."

"Probably," Jonathan agreed, wincing as he felt the bruised place where Vince had kicked him. "He's not the nicest kid I've ever known."

Mr. Bruce made a clucking sound with his tongue. "And look," he said, "Charlie bit you, too. Your ankle's bleeding."

Sure enough, a thin trickle of blood was running down Jonathan's ankle, staining his white sock with red.

"That's okay," Jonathan told his neighbor. "It doesn't hurt. That is, Charlie has had his rabies shots, hasn't he?"

"Oh, yes," Mr. Bruce assured him quickly. "Every one of them. Still, I'm sorry this happened. I'm sure Charlie was aiming at the other boy and just got you by mistake."

"I wish he'd gotten him, too," Jonathan said. "Vince needs to know what it feels like to get hurt, for a change." He looked at his watch. "Oh, no, school starts in fifteen minutes! If I don't hurry, I'm going to be late. Good-bye, Mr. Bruce, and don't worry, I'm okay."

Mr. Bruce stooped to help Jonathan pick up his books and homework.

"You can't go until I've cleaned that ankle and put some antiseptic on it," he said firmly. "Looks like you could use a bandage, too. And I want to give you lunch money for today. It's a sure thing you can't eat *that*." He pointed to the mess on the sidewalk.

"Thanks." Jonathan limped through the gate and up Mr. Bruce's sidewalk, following the old man. "But then I really will have to hurry, Mr. Bruce."

Five minutes later, Jonathan pushed the gate open again, darting a worried glance at his watch. Maybe he should cut across that big vacant lot on Mulberry Street. He could save a minute or two that way.

"Wait!"

Jonathan stopped and spun around to stare at the old man. "Yes?" he said, trying not to sound impatient.

"Charlie's had his shots, all right," Mr. Bruce said. Was it Jonathan's imagination, or was the man's expression suddenly strange? "But you've got to promise, if you start feeling—oh, weird or sick or funny, promise you'll let me know, okay?"

Jonathan stared at him.

"Okay," he said. "I guess. But why should I feel funny? It's just a little bite."

Mr. Bruce tried to smile, but somehow his smile didn't look quite right.

"I'm sure you'll be just fine," he said. "But I'd feel better if you'd promise. Just humor an old man, son, all right?"

Jonathan shrugged. "Sure," he said. "But don't worry about me. I'm fine. Really. I have to go now, okay? See you later. See you, Charlie."

With a last wave, Jonathan turned and raced down the street. If he was late, he'd have to spend fifteen minutes in the principal's office after school. That was the last thing he needed.

CHAPTER FOUR

Something Going Around

By first recess, Jonathan was starting to feel a little funny. Quietly, so Mrs. Young wouldn't notice, he stuck one hand underneath his T-shirt and scratched his stomach. Why did his skin suddenly feel so itchy? No matter how hard he scratched, it felt the same way it did back in second grade when he had chicken pox. But you couldn't get chicken pox again, could you?

At recess, he went to the boys' room to check, just in case. Locking himself in one of the stalls, he lifted his shirt and looked, There were none of the little red spots he remembered from the chicken pox. There wasn't even a rash, but his skin felt as if it were on fire. And now the itching had spread to his arms, his back, and his legs.

Maybe it was something he had eaten, he decided, as he went out to the playground to meet Tony and the rest of the gang on the jungle gym. The itching would probably go away soon.

But he felt even worse after recess. The classroom felt chilly, but none of the other kids were shivering or putting on their sweaters. The funny thing was, the coldest part of Jonathan was his nose. He touched it and jerked his hand away in surprise. His nose wasn't just cold, it was wet! Oh, great, he thought, eyeing the box of tissues on Mrs. Young's desk. Now he was going to have a runny nose on top of everything else. That was really all he needed.

"Jonathan?" Mrs. Young was watching

him with a worried look on her face. "Jonathan, do you feel okay? You look kind of funny."

"No, I'm fine," he answered, even though his mouth felt strange and stiff, as if it couldn't shape itself around his words. "I'm—I'm just a little cold, that's all."

"Really?" She frowned. "That's funny, it feels plenty warm in here to me."

Jonathan nodded, reaching quietly to scratch an especially itchy place on his right ankle.

It didn't help any that Vince the Vampire had been glaring across the room at him all morning. Jonathan shivered when he thought how mad the bully must be. He was probably already making plans to get even with Jonathan for fighting back that morning. Jonathan wouldn't dare let Vince catch him alone for a few days, anyway.

"Mrs. Young, Mrs. Young!" That was Cissy, the prissy girl who sat just across the aisle from Jonathan. "Mrs. Young,

Jonathan is sticking out his tongue at me!"

Mrs. Young turned around from the blackboard. "Honestly, Jonathan!" she said sternly. "I don't know how you behaved in your old school, but around here we don't do things like that."

Jonathan stared at her, too surprised to answer. "But I wasn't sticking my tongue out!" he argued. "Honest, Mrs. Young, I didn't do it."

"He did, too," Cissy piped up. "His tongue was hanging halfway out of his mouth."

"Look!" Vince the Vampire had to butt in. "He's doing it again, Mrs. Young."

"I am not!" Jonathan started to say, but he couldn't, because his tongue really *was* hanging from his mouth, almost to the bottom of his chin. Quickly, he jerked it back where it belonged and snapped his mouth shut. How had *that* happened?

Mrs. Young heaved a tired sigh. "Really, Jonathan," she said, "this doesn't seem like you at all. I'm tempted to send you to the principal's office—and I would, too, except that you've never done anything like this before. Consider this your final warning. One more time and I'll march you down the hall to the office myself. Understood?"

"Yes, Mrs. Young," Jonathan mumbled miserably, his face burning.

He kept his eyes glued to the top of his desk while all the other kids whispered, giggled, and pointed. It seemed like a million years until lunchtime.

In the cafeteria, all the kids groaned when they saw what old Mrs. Peaveley, the school cook, was ladling onto their trays. Liver and onions, yuck!

"No complaining," the cook told them grumpily. "It's Nutrition Week, remember? Liver has lots of iron in it, and it's good for you. So be quiet and eat."

Great, Jonathan thought gloomily. And if Vince hadn't mashed his lunch into the sidewalk, he could have had that yummy lunch Mom had packed this morning.

Now he was stuck with liver and onions!

Then something *really* weird happened. Holding his nose, Jonathan forked the first slimy piece of liver into his mouth. He expected to gag, the way he always did when Mom made him eat liver. But to his amazement, the liver didn't taste quite as disgusting as usual. In fact, he decided, as he gulped down another piece, this stuff was actually pretty good. Maybe Mom could get Mrs. Peaveley's recipe. Smacking his lips, he tried a third piece, and a fourth, and each bite tasted better than the one before it.

Suddenly, he noticed that all the kids at his table had gotten quiet. Looking up, he saw that Alyssa and Patrick and the others were staring at him, their eyes wide, as he gobbled the rest of his liver and scraped the last bit of gravy from his plate.

"Gosh, Jonathan, you—you really *like* that stuff?" Tony asked, his eyes almost bugging out of his head.

Jonathan stared at his empty plate.

"Not usually," he said. "But it wasn't really bad, for liver."

The other kids exchanged glances.

"I don't suppose you want to eat mine, do you?" Tony asked, shoving his plate toward Jonathan.

"You can have mine, too," Alyssa offered generously.

"And mine," added Roger and Jennifer and the others.

"Hey, you guys, I can't eat all that!" Jonathan protested as they piled his plate high with liver and onions.

But then he took a bite, and a few minutes later, his plate was clean again.

"I can't believe it," Roger said, shaking his head. "You can sit next to me *anytime* we have liver, Jonathan."

Jonathan was too full of liver and onions to play on the jungle gym after lunch. So he just sat on a playground bench, cupping one hand around his chilly, wet nose and using the other to chase itchy places.

If he didn't feel any better by tomorrow, he'd have to ask Mom to call the doctor, just in case. He probably had something that was going around.

And he scratched his stomach again.

CHAPTER FIVE

By the
Light of the Moon

By the end of the school day, Jonathan was sure that he was getting sick. Now, in addition to the itching and the wet nose, something was wrong with his throat. It didn't hurt, exactly, but his voice sounded weirder every time he talked. In fact, just before the last bell, when Mrs. Young asked him when the Pilgrims landed at Plymouth Rock, the sound that came out of Jonathan's mouth made everyone turn and stare.

"Gosh, Jonathan," Jennifer said with a giggle, "what's the matter with your voice? You almost sound like a dog howling."

"Maybe you'd better gargle some hot salt water when you get home," Mrs. Young suggested. "You could be getting a sore throat."

As if all that weren't enough, Jonathan had to slink home by back alleys and side streets. He didn't like the way Vince the Vampire looked at him just before the bell. Maybe the bully wouldn't follow him if he sneaked home a different way. He only hoped Vince wouldn't be waiting on his front porch.

There was no sign of the enemy when Jonathan finally slipped in through the backyard. Quickly, he unlocked the door to his house and hurried inside, locking the door and putting on the chain. At least this wasn't one of Mom's late nights, so he wouldn't be alone for long.

He tried gargling hot salt water, but it didn't seem to help. His throat still felt funny, and his skin was itching worse than ever.

Well, he told himself, look on the bright side. If you've caught something, you'll have to stay home from school tomorrow. At least that way you won't have to face Vince for a couple of days.

He wasn't hungry for supper that night. Maybe it was all that liver he had eaten for lunch. But somehow Mom's vegetarian lasagna didn't look very good.

"I think you'd better go to bed," his mother suggested, laying a hand on his forehead. "Funny, you don't seem to have a fever. But you don't look very good. Why don't you make it an early night?"

"I think I will," Jonathan agreed. "I'll probably feel better in the morning."

Lying in bed, staring at the glow of the streetlights on his bedroom ceiling, Jonathan suddenly remembered Mr. Bruce, and the strange things he had said this morning about how Jonathan should tell him if he started to feel funny. How did he know I was catching something?

Jonathan wondered. Maybe I was already starting to look sick. Oh, well. I'll tell him later, when I'm feeling better. He wouldn't expect me to get out of bed and go next door to tell him now.

Jonathan's alarm clock said 3:14 in the morning when he awoke suddenly, his heart pounding, his mouth dry, and his head spinning dizzily. Oh, he thought groggily, I really am sick. Maybe I'd better call Mom.

He opened his mouth to yell, but all that came out was a funny yipping sound. Clearing his throat, he tried again. This time it sounded more like a howl.

Great, he thought. Laryngitis. Just what I need.

Suddenly he noticed something that made his heart hammer in his ears. A full yellow moon had risen, and its bright rays fell straight over Jonathan's bed, making his room almost as light as day. Jonathan could see very clearly where his legs should have been, making bumps under the blankets. Only they weren't. The blankets were mussed and wrinkled, but there was no sign of his legs. Or his stomach, or his arms, or—

With a funny groaning sound, Jonathan reached down to slap at the empty bed, feeling for his legs as if they were hiding down there somewhere. Then, as he caught sight of his hand in the moonlight, he gasped. It wasn't his hand! He was patting the blankets with something small and round and fuzzy, something white and hairy that looked like—like—

A paw! A dog's paw! Where was his hand, and where had he gotten a dog's paw?

By this time Jonathan was wide awake. Kicking the covers to the bottom of the bed, he looked down at himself, and his heart stopped for a second. From head to foot, his body had shrunk and changed shape—and grown a thick coat of curly white hair. What was even worse, craning his neck around, he caught sight of something sticking up at the end of his back,

something that looked suspiciously like a tail. And now he saw his blue-and-white-striped pajamas lying in a crumpled heap in the middle of his bed, as if—as if—as if he had suddenly gotten so small that they had simply fallen off him!

This can't be happening, Jonathan told himself, trying to calm the frantic beating of his heart. It's all just a bad dream. Any minute now I'll wake up, and then—

But the minutes crawled by, and Jonathan didn't wake up. When the glowing numbers of his alarm clock read 4:00, he couldn't take it anymore. He had to see for himself. He had to find out. He had to—

He tried to swing his legs over the side of the bed, and almost fell before he remembered how short his legs had become. It looked like a mile to the floor, but he took a deep breath, shut his eyes, and launched himself out into space, landing with a thud.

The moon was about to set, but there was still enough light for Jonathan to see himself in the full-length mirror that hung on his closet door. And what he saw made him whimper and shake all over.

Staring at him from the mirror was a little, curly-haired white poodle, just like Charlie next door. Jonathan blinked in disbelief, and the poodle in the mirror blinked back. Jonathan lifted one paw to his eyes to block out the terrible sight, and so did the poodle. Jonathan bared his teeth in a growl, and the poodle bared sharp white teeth back at him.

"No," Jonathan whispered. "No. This can't be happening." But his voice was a frightened whine.

Trembling from head to tail, Jonathan crawled into his closet, where he lay on an old bathrobe that had fallen from its hanger. It seemed like forever that he huddled there, shaking, scared, and miserable. But before morning he must have dropped back to sleep, because he was awakened by the loud buzzing of his alarm clock.

Sleepily, he brushed the hair from his

eyes and rolled over to shut off the alarm. Then he realized where he was.

"What am I doing in the closet?" he mumbled grumpily.

And then he remembered.

But it was a dream. It must have been. Because there were his feet, and his hands, and his legs. And when he went to look at himself in the mirror, his usual face stared back at him.

He was wrapped up in his old bathrobe, and he could see his pajamas crumpled up in his bed. But there—there on the floor, just a few inches away . . .

Hardly daring to breathe, Jonathan reached out and picked it up. It was a tiny wisp of white, curly hair. Poodle hair.

Jonathan gulped as he realized he'd just spent the night as a poodle!

CHAPTER SIX

Not Again!

Jonathan had trouble concentrating in school that day. As if it hadn't been bad enough having to sneak to school to avoid Vince the Vampire, now he had even worse problems on his mind. While Mrs. Young talked about long division and remainders, Jonathan worried about what had occurred the night before. As she explained prepositions and conjunctions, he thought about what *might* happen *tonight*. He had a funny feeling that he just might wake up tomorrow morning in the closet again. And that could be a real disaster, because tomorrow was Saturday, so Mom wouldn't be rushing around getting ready for work. She might even peek into his room to see what he wanted for Saturday breakfast. And if she saw him curled up on the closet floor, all hairy and dog-shaped . . . Jonathan didn't even want to think about it.

In the first place, what if she shooed him out the front door before he'd had a chance to change back into a boy? Then, because Jonathan the boy wasn't in his room, she'd probably think he had been kidnapped or something, and there'd be police all over the place. That was the last thing Jonathan needed.

Even worse, what if she saw him *while* he was changing back? At the very least, she would scream and faint. Then she'd probably insist on rushing him to the emergency room to find out what was wrong with him. And what was he supposed to tell the doctors—"Don't worry, it's perfectly okay, I just seem to be changing into a werepoodle"? Yeah. Sure.

Jonathan decided he would have to think of some way to keep Mom from finding out. He worried about it all through lunch and noon recess. Maybe he could tell his mother that he'd been invited to spend the night at Tony's house. In fact, he could call her at the office and be gone before she even got home. She'd probably want to call Tony's mom, just to make sure, but he'd talk her out of that somehow. Maybe he could say that Tony's phone was out of order. Then he could spend the night in the storage shed in the backyard and not come home again until he had completely finished changing back in the morning. Of course, it would be awfully cold out in the shed in the middle of November, but he could take his sleeping bag and a pile of old blankets with him. Not to mention the fact that by the time the moon rose he'd probably be covered all over with thick white fur.

If he really *did* change into a poodle tonight, of course. Now he wished he'd paid closer attention to that werewolf movie. Did the guy transform every night, or just when the moon was full? Jonathan decided he couldn't take any chances.

The moon was just past full that night, but it was still round and bright as it rose over the roof of the Andersens' garage. Jonathan held his breath and stared at the back of his hand. Would it happen, now that the moon was no longer full? Maybe the whole thing had just been a crazy dream. Maybe—

And then he saw it—a little wisp of curly white hair on the back of his hand.

"No!" he gasped. "Not again!"

There was more hair crawling up his arm, and down his stomach, and across his neck. At the same time, he felt himself getting smaller and smaller, until his clothes seemed to swallow him up. Giving

himself a shake, he crawled out of his suddenly enormous sweatshirt, hearing his glasses clatter to the floor, and stood in a patch of moonlight that fell across the shed floor, a little white poodle.

"No," he moaned again, but this time it came out more like "Woooooo!"

Suddenly, it didn't seem like enough just to hide out here until morning. He had to find out *why* he was changing into a poodle. He glanced at the house next door. Suddenly, he remembered Mr. Bruce's words after Charlie bit him. "But you've got to promise, if you start feeling— oh, weird or sick or funny, promise you'll let me know, okay?"

Mr. Bruce must have known all along that this might happen, thought Jonathan, or he wouldn't have said that about me feeling funny. But how did he know? Had this happened before, to some other kid? And if so, would Mr. Bruce know how to get him back to normal again?

The only thing to do was to get over to Mr. Bruce's house as fast as he could. So

Not Again!

Jonathan stuck his furry head out the shed door, peering about to make sure no one was around. Then he trotted on his four hairy feet across the backyard, to a spot where he knew there was a hole in the hedge between his yard and Mr. Bruce's. The hole was plenty big enough for him now, and he didn't even snag his fur on the bare branches as he scooted through. Then he ran up the back walk to Mr. Bruce's kitchen door, his toenails clicking on the concrete every step of the way.

Guess I forgot just one tiny detail, Jonathan thought as he scrambled up the steps to the back porch. I can't knock on the door, and I can't call for Mr. Bruce to let me in either. Now what? Think, Jonathan. How does Charlie let Mr. Bruce know when he needs to come in?

Jonathan felt like a real idiot as he threw his head back, pointed his little black nose at the sky, took a deep breath, and let out a shrill, piercing howl. If that didn't bring Mr. Bruce to the door, nothing would.

CHAPTER SEVEN

Lost: One Chewbone

Sure enough, a few seconds later Jonathan heard footsteps inside the house. The porch light went on, and Mr. Bruce parted the curtains on the kitchen door. His eyes grew wide and his mouth made an O of surprise as he looked down and saw Jonathan. Then he fumbled with the lock and threw the door open.

"Oh, no!" Jonathan heard him moan. "I was hoping it wouldn't come to this.

Jonathan, that's you, isn't it? If it is, bark three times, please."

"Ruff!" Jonathan barked grumpily. "Ruff! Ruff!"

"It *is* you." Mr. Bruce shook his head sadly. "I can't tell you how sorry I am that this happened. Quickly, boy, let's get you inside before anyone sees you out here."

Bending down, he scooped Jonathan into his arms. For a second, Jonathan thought he might throw up. It was like being on a very fast elevator. Did pets feel like this every time people picked them up? Then Mr. Bruce hurried into the warm kitchen and shut the door behind them.

"You're half-frozen," the old man muttered. "How long have you been outside? Never mind, I forgot that you can't answer. Here, let's put you over by the woodstove so you can thaw out. Charlie! Charlemagne, you bad dog, get yourself in here and see what you've done now!"

Jonathan heard the rapid clicking of toenails on the floor as Charlie hurried down the hall toward the kitchen. An instant later, Charlie skidded to a halt, his little black eyes bugging out as he saw the other poodle.

"Jonathan!" Charlie yapped. "Jonathan, is that you?"

"Wait a minute!" Jonathan yapped back. "I understood you! I understood every word you said. How could I do that? You're a dog!"

"So are you, in case you haven't noticed," Charlie answered, sniffing him nose to nose. "You'll find that during your times as a werepoodle, you'll be able to understand anything a dog says—any dog. Why should that surprise you? People can understand people, can't they? Although, to be fair, I can remember being surprised the first time it happened to me, too."

"Tell him about it, Charlie," Mr. Bruce said, from his chair near the stove.

Startled, Jonathan swerved to stare up at him. Could Mr. Bruce understand dog talk, too?

The old man must have caught his surprised glance. "No, Jonathan," he said, "I can't understand a word you and Charlie are saying. But I think I know what you're talking about. And you did the right thing by coming here. Charlie is the only one who has the answers you need. I only hope he can help. You see, Charlie used to be a human, too."

"What?" Now Jonathan stared at the other dog. "You mean this has happened to people before? You weren't always a poodle?"

Charlie shook his head, making his white topknot dance. "Certainly not," he replied. "I used to be a mailman, walking around town in the rain and the heat and the ice, hauling sacks full of heavy packages and bills and advertisements. Until one day a little white poodle ran out from one of the houses on my route and took a bite out of my ankle. The next time the moon was full, I turned into a poodle. I remember how upset I was at first. I hated

57

switching back and forth—mailman, poodle, mailman, poodle. That just about drove me crazy."

Jonathan nodded. "I know just what you mean," he said. "So how come you're not still switching back and forth? How come you're a dog in the daytime, too?"

Charlie sighed and flopped down on the kitchen rug, laying his head on his shaggy paws.

"There's a catch to this whole werepoodle business," he warned Jonathan. "It's not the way it is in the movies, where the man never changes into a wolf unless the moon is full. A person can change into a poodle for several nights every month, just as long as the moon is still round. It's round right now, which is why you changed tonight. But after a while, you—well, you just forget how to change back, I guess. Then you have to stay a poodle forever. That's what happened to me. One morning I just stayed a poodle. That was years and years ago, and I've been a poodle ever since." He looked up at Mr. Bruce, and his fluffy white tail thumped on the floor. "Lucky for me, Mr. Bruce found me running the streets, and he took me in. Mr. Bruce is not an ordinary man, Jonathan. I think in the olden days they would have called him a wizard."

"A wizard!" Jonathan looked at the old man in the rocking chair. Who would have guessed? And yet, there was something strange about Mr. Bruce, now that he thought about it—that flowing white hair, the long snowy beard, and the way he always wore black. Maybe it wasn't so hard to believe after all. "You mean he casts spells and makes magic brews and all that stuff?"

Charlie laughed a soft doggy laugh.

"Not that kind of wizard," he said. "But he understands about things like werepoodles, and he knew right away that I wasn't an ordinary dog. He has—oh, I guess you'd call it a kind of sixth sense about things

like that. Anyway, he took me in, and he's taken care of me all this time. Otherwise I might have ended up in the pound long ago."

"But that's a terrible story!" Jonathan cried. "All these years, and you haven't been able to get your own body back? How can you stand it?"

Charlie looked surprised. "It's not that terrible once you get used to it," he said. "Actually, I don't think I'd want to go back to being a mailman. I used to get terrible backaches from lugging all those packages, and my feet were always cold and wet in the winter. Not to mention that now I don't have to pay bills or cut the grass or buy groceries. Don't waste your time feeling sorry for me, Jonathan. I'm fine the way I am. I'm just sorry I landed you in such a mess. I really didn't mean to bite you, you know. I was aiming for that big, obnoxious Vince kid, the one who was picking on you. On him fur would have looked good."

Jonathan sighed. "I know you didn't mean to," he said. "It's okay, Charlie, honest. I'm not mad. But I've been feeling so awful the last two days, I haven't known what to do. I think I'll go nuts if I have to go on like this. First my skin started itching like crazy—"

Charlie nodded. "That's your new fur growing in," he explained. "The itch gets better after a while, but it is pretty bad at first. What else?"

"Well, my nose is always wet," Jonathan told him.

"Dogs' noses are always wet," Charlie said. "They're supposed to be. Don't worry, you'll get used to it. Anything else?"

Jonathan thought a minute. "Well, I ate everyone's liver and onions at school yesterday," he remembered. "And I usually hate liver."

"*You* hate liver," Charlie said. "Dogs *love* it. And I bet your voice was getting all weird, too, right? Like a dog's howl? Well, that's normal, too. I went through all those things when I first changed, so I know how you feel."

"But there must be something we can do," Jonathan begged. "Maybe it's okay for you, but I don't *want* to stay a poodle forever. I want to grow up and go to college and be a jet pilot. And my mom needs me. She'll be scared to death if I never come back. I just can't do that to her. There must be some way I can keep this from happening!"

Charlie nodded. "There is," he said. "Mr. Bruce discovered the cure years ago. It was too late for me, but the change is just starting for you. I think we still have time."

"Great!" Jonathan jumped to all four feet with an excited little yelp. "What do I have to do? I'll do anything!"

Charlie and Mr. Bruce exchanged long, anxious glances, and suddenly Jonathan felt a worried little shiver run down his furry back.

"What is it?" he demanded. "What is it, Charlie? Is there a problem?"

"Well, yes, there is, a little one," Charlie admitted. "You see, Mr. Bruce knew from his reading that there's a plant called wolf-bane that can change werewolves back to people. He thinks it will work for werepoodles, too, if you catch them soon enough. In fact, he actually made a big chewbone out of the stuff, so all you would have to do is chew on it a little. The trouble is— well—" The little dog fidgeted uneasily.

"*What?*" Jonathan yipped. "What is it?"

Charlie took a deep breath. "Mr. Bruce kept the chewbone with all the rest of his magic stuff, out in the garage," he explained. "One day last week, he didn't quite get the garage door closed, and another dog got in. We looked out the kitchen window just in time to see the big fleabag run off with the chewbone in his mouth."

"What?" Jonathan exploded. "And you mean you didn't go after it? What kind of watchdog are you?"

"A little one," Charlie reminded him. "And it was an awfully big dog."

"I can tell by the way you're yipping that Charlie just told you the bad news," Mr. Bruce interrupted. "I guess we should have tried to get the chewbone back, but by that time I had decided we'd probably never need the thing. After all, it was too late for Charlie, and I didn't really expect to run into the situation again. How often do you meet a werepoodle?"

"But do you know where the chewbone is now?" Jonathan yelped. "Did Mr. Bruce recognize the dog that took it?"

Charlie nodded. "As a matter of fact, he did," he answered. "He even knows where the dog lives. But you're not going to like it."

"What's the dog's name?" Jonathan asked. "And who does he belong to?"

"His name is Big Al," Charlie said gloomily. "And I'm afraid you don't get along with his master."

Jonathan gasped. "You don't mean, you can't mean—"

Charlie nodded. "It's that obnoxious

Vince kid. The one you call the Vampire. Big Al is his dog. To change you back into a boy permanently, we're going to have to get that chewbone back from Big Al. If he hasn't chewed it into a million bits by now, of course."

"But couldn't Mr. Bruce make another one?" Jonathan suggested. "How hard could it be to make a little chewbone?"

"You're forgetting one thing," Charlie reminded him. "It's a magic chewbone, made out of wolfbane, which you can't exactly buy at the supermarket. It took months for Mr. Bruce to come up with enough of it to make the first bone. It's a very rare plant. And unfortunately, Jonathan, you don't have months."

Jonathan stared at him. "What—what do you mean?" he whispered in a strangled voice. "How long do I have?"

Charlie looked him straight in the eye. "You have until the moon turns, two nights from now," he said. "As long as the moon is round, you're okay. But after that, it's too late. If we don't have that chew-bone by then, you'll be a poodle forever."

Jonathan felt the kitchen spinning around him, and suddenly Charlie was nothing but a white, fuzzy blur. Then the whole world went as black as a moonless night, as black as a poodle's nose.

CHAPTER EIGHT

Big Al

"I'm glad you had such a good time at Tony's last night," Mom said, taking the vacuum cleaner and the mop bucket from the kitchen closet. "It's about time you started making friends here. His phone must have been fixed, by the way. I tried calling his mother, but the number was busy. I'm surprised you came home this early. I thought you'd probably hang around with Tony for a while."

"He, uh—he had to go shopping with

his mother," Jonathan answered, his head spinning. That had been a close call. What if Mom really had spoken to Tony's mother? "We'll probably do something later. My room's clean now, Mom. Is it okay if I go out for a while?"

"Where?" Mom's voice sounded muffled, because she had stuck her head into the closet again, looking for the furniture polish. "And when will you be back?"

"There's a kid in class I want to go see," Jonathan explained. "I won't be long. I just have to ask him something."

"What kid?" Mom asked.

"You don't know him," he answered. "His name is Vince."

He hurried through the kitchen, pushing his arms through the sleeves of his jacket as he went.

Out in the street, he turned the corner and headed down Zinnia, and then made a left turn onto Hollyhock. Mr. Bruce had found Vince's address in the phone book and had told Jonathan how to get there.

"But I'll get squashed like a bug if Vince sees me hanging around his house!" Jonathan had argued. He had just finished changing back to a boy, and he was still feeling a little weird and woozy, which made him grumpy. Besides, he hadn't gotten much rest all night, sleeping on the floor in front of the woodstove with Charlie.

"So try not to let Vince see you," Mr. Bruce advised him. "The important thing is to find out what his dog did with the chewbone. If you see it, grab it. Then our troubles will be over."

"How am I supposed to know it's the right chewbone?" Jonathan asked. "And what makes you think it isn't all chewed up by now, anyway?"

"You won't have any trouble recognizing it," his neighbor promised. "It's probably the only bright green chewbone in the world. And I don't think Big Al could have chewed it all up this soon. For one thing, I made it extra-big. For another thing, it's very hard. Any dog would need time to work his way through it. You probably ought to look inside Big Al's doghouse. That's where I'd hide a chewbone, if I were a dog."

Jonathan's heart pounded in his chest as he reached the corner and checked the address on the house. This was the right place, all right—103 Hollyhock. Jonathan had been expecting a big, gloomy old house with towers and stained-glass windows and a black iron fence, the kind of place where someone named Vince the Vampire would feel at home. But Vince's house was ordinary-looking, with a white picket fence and a yard full of flowerbeds that would be filled with color in the spring. It didn't seem at all like a place a vampire would live.

Hiding behind a big old maple tree, Jonathan peered one way, then another, checking for any sign of the bully or his dog. Vince didn't seem to be anywhere around. He was probably out pushing little kids down and taking their candy. But there in the side yard, near a small garage, was a snug-looking doghouse. And there, snoozing with his head propped on his paws, lay the biggest basset hound Jonathan had ever seen. The dog's face and ears were so long and droopy, they looked as if they were melting. Even from the street, Jonathan could hear the dog's rumbling snore.

This was Big Al? Jonathan had expected a Doberman, or a chow, or a German shepherd at the very least. Big Al didn't look mean enough to bite an earthworm. Maybe getting a peek inside the doghouse wouldn't be so hard after all. If Jonathan could just get into the yard without being caught.

This is a snap! he thought as he eased the gate silently open. There didn't even seem to be anyone home. Now all he had to do was tiptoe over to the doghouse, make up to that droopy, lazy-looking dog, and check the doghouse for the chewbone.

72

If he found it, he could be out of the yard in ten seconds, tops.

As Jonathan crept closer to the dog-house, his heart beat faster. He had seen a flash of something bright green in the dead grass, right underneath Big Al's huge paw. The chewbone? It had to be! Right out there in plain sight, too. How easy could this be?

But as Jonathan bent down and slowly, gently eased his hand out to take the chew-bone, Big Al's head snapped up, and his eyes flew open. "Rrrrrrrrr," he rumbled in his chest.

"Shh, boy," Jonathan whispered, "I'm not going to hurt anything. Just let me have a look at that chewbone, okay? Atta-boy. Just a second, there—"

"Woof!" Big Al jumped to his feet, and suddenly the silence was split with a string of deafening barks. "Woof! Woof! Woof!"

"Hush," Jonathan said, looking desper-ately over his shoulder. "What are you try-ing to do, get me killed? I told you, all I want is—"

But Big Al took one menacing step toward him, and then another, baring his teeth. Jonathan began backing toward the safety of the gate.

Then he heard the front door of the house fly open. "Who's there?" someone yelled. Jonathan groaned to himself as he recognized Vince's voice. "Hey, who told you you could hang around here, Four-Eyes? You aren't trying to steal any of our stuff, are you? Sure, I bet that's what you're doing. I ought to call the police, or maybe I should just sic my dog on you!"

"Please, Vince," Jonathan begged, "I wasn't going to steal anything, honest. I was just—"

The bully had charged down the porch steps, and now he was stalking toward Jonathan, his face red and his fists clenched.

"You'd better beat it," he snarled, "or—" He shook a fist at Jonathan.

"You got it," Jonathan agreed. "I'm out of here. Just don't let your dog chase me, okay?"

And he backed all the way down the walk, never daring to turn his back on the furious Vince or his growling dog until he was through the gate. Out on the sidewalk, he ran faster than he had ever run in his life, not slowing down until he had reached Apple Street.

He turned in at Mr. Bruce's gate, marched up the walk, and rang the doorbell. He hoped the old man would have some ideas. Because if he didn't . . .

Jonathan had checked the calendar that morning. And Charlie was right, soon the moon would be shrinking. There were only two more nights for Jonathan to get that chewbone.

Otherwise, he might as well ask Mom now if she could get him a new flea collar for Christmas.

CHAPTER NINE

Shark Attack!

The moon was a huge silver coin above the trees as Jonathan and Charlie trotted down the sidewalk toward Vince's house, their toenails clicking like tiny castanets. The night was chilly, and the little dogs' breath hung in silvery plumes in front of their shaggy faces.

"At least the moon's still round," Charlie yipped. "We still have some time."

"Not long," Jonathan answered. "Tomorrow is the last night. After that—" He didn't finish. He didn't have to.

Charlie looked at him out of the corners of his bright black eyes. "There's something else bothering you, too," he said. "Whatever it is, you might as well tell me."

Jonathan sighed a doggy sigh. "I've been worried all day," he admitted. "You see, when I—when I changed back this morning, I don't think I changed all the way. There was still some white fur between my toes. And my voice sounded weirder than ever. Mom made me take the most disgusting cough medicine. I could be wrong, but I think my ears aren't quite right either. At least, they look a little pointy to me. I had to comb my hair right down over them so Mom wouldn't see. I'm scared, Charlie. I think it's starting to happen already. I'm changing into a dog, and it's getting harder and harder to change back."

"Nothing permanent can happen as long as the moon is round," Charlie reassured him. "You'll be okay. By the way, where did you tell your mother you were going tonight?"

"To Roger's house," Jonathan said. "I hate lying to her so much, but what choice do I have? Anyway, she's so happy I'm making new friends, she doesn't ask a lot of questions. But I don't know what she'll do after tomorrow if—if . . ." He swallowed hard.

"Try not to think about it," Charlie said gently. "Mr. Bruce had a good idea. Maybe Big Al will listen to us if we tell him why you need the chewbone. At least you can talk to him now. It's not like this morning."

"I don't even know how we're going to get into Vince's yard," Jonathan pointed out, as they turned the corner onto Hollyhock. "There's a fence all the way round it, see?"

Charlie just chuckled. "Didn't you listen to Mr. Bruce?" he asked. "There's never been a fence made yet that I can't dig my way under."

Sure enough, a few minutes later both poodles were able to squeeze their way through a neatly dug hole and into the side yard where Big Al's doghouse stood. Even from the edge of the yard, they could hear the basset hound's rumbling snores.

"I thought he was a real pussycat when I first saw him," Jonathan whispered. "But for such a big, lazy-looking dog, he sure can move fast. Are you sure he won't bite our heads off first and ask questions later?"

"Leave it to me," Charlie answered. "I've been a dog long enough to know how to handle Big Al."

As they trotted up to the doghouse, Big Al snorted, shook his head, and opened bleary-looking eyes.

"Wha—" he snuffled. "What are you two doing here?" Then, suddenly, he came all the way awake. "Hey!" he growled, jumping to his feet. "Get out of my yard, you dust mops, before I sweep the place with you!"

Jonathan was already backing his way toward the hole under the fence, but Charlie held his ground.

"Not so fast," he said calmly. "Give us a break, Big Al. We're not here to bother anything. We just want to pass the time a little, and maybe make a deal with you."

"A deal?" The basset hound glared suspiciously at them from his wrinkled face. "What kind of deal? A deal for what?"

Charlie jerked his head toward Jonathan, who stood in the shadows, trembling a little.

"My friend Jonathan was here yesterday," he said. "You may remember him—a boy about nine years old, glasses, dark hair, blue jeans?"

Big Al stared through the darkness toward Jonathan. *"That's* the kid who was here this morning?" he asked. "Yeah, I thought he smelled familiar. He's the one who was trying to take my chewbone. I remember, all right. But wait a minute. If he was a kid this morning, how come he's a dog tonight?"

Charlie sighed. "It's a long story," he said. "Maybe we'd all better sit down while I explain."

A few minutes later, as Charlie finished his explanation, Big Al shook his head, making his ears flop from side to side.

"I've heard all those stories about people changing into dogs," he admitted. "But I never knew they were true. And you say it was all because you were trying to bite my Vince, huh?"

"Only because he was picking on Jonathan," Charlie reminded him quickly. "You may love your human, Big Al, but frankly, you haven't trained him too well."

Big Al lay down and hung his head. "It's true," he said in an embarrassed voice. "I love the kid, but he still needs a lot of work. So anyway, let me see if I got it right. The kid here needs my chewbone or he's a dog forever, is that it?"

"Well, it's not even really your chew

bone, if you want to get technical," Charlie said. "Don't forget, you took it from Mr. Bruce's garage in the first place."

"Oh, yeah," Big Al mumbled, "I forgot. Well, kid, I wish I could let you have the chewbone, but I can't. No way. Sorry."

"What!" Charlie yapped impatiently.

"Come on, Big Al," Jonathan begged, "let's not play games, okay? This is my whole *life* we're talking about here."

"Simmer down, okay?" Big Al lifted one huge paw. "I said I'd give you the chewbone if I could, and I meant it. But the fact is, I—uh—I've lost the chewbone myself."

"You *what?*" the little dogs barked in chorus.

Big Al squirmed. He seemed to have trouble getting the words out. "Well, it's like this," he said at last. "When Vince went off to the park yesterday, he left the gate open a little. I don't get out of the yard much, so naturally I couldn't pass up such a great chance to explore the neighborhood. And I shouldn't have done it, maybe, but—well, I took the chewbone with me, just in case I was in the mood to have a little nibble."

"And you dropped it somewhere!" Jonathan guessed. "Oh, this is just great! Any dog in town could have it now! Do you at least remember where you might have dropped it?"

"I didn't say I dropped it, boy," Big Al rumbled, drawing his forehead up in an annoyed pucker. "Give a guy a chance to finish explaining, okay? No, what happened was, I decided to go down to the city dump and nose around a little. Sometimes a dog can find some really good stuff at the dump. I'd forgotten about Shark."

"Shark?" Jonathan echoed, puzzled.

"Oh, no!" Charlie gasped. "Don't tell me you ran into Shark!" He turned to Jonathan. "Sharp is the meanest dog in town," he explained. "He lives at the dump. I think he belongs to the night watchman there. Anyway, his name fits him perfectly. That's all you have to know about Shark."

He turned back to Big Al. "I'm starting to have a very bad feeling about this," he said. "You're about to tell us that Shark took the chewbone, right?"

Big Al nodded sadly, making his long ears jiggle. "You got it," he said. "He jumped out at me from behind some old tires. I didn't even see him coming. See where he bit me, right here on my left shoulder? Anyway, the next thing I knew, I was picking myself up from a pile of old tin cans, and Shark was running off with my—your—chewbone."

"But this is awful!" Jonathan cried. "We've got to go after this Shark character and get that chewbone back! Now, this very minute!"

But Charlie and Big Al were both staring at him, shaking their heads slowly from side to side.

"You don't understand, Jonathan," Charlie said. "Shark is about twice the size of Big Al here. And he eats little dogs like us for breakfast. He would if he could get ahold of us, anyway. We can't just go after him and snatch the chewbone back. We'll have to use our brains."

"But we don't have time for that!" Jonathan argued, feeling more panicked by the second. "The moon is shrinking. After tomorrow night, it won't be round anymore. And then it will be too late. I'll be a dog forever!"

"Wait a minute!" Big Al interrupted. "It may sound crazy, but I think I know how you can get your chewbone back. Listen, you guys. You're not going to like this, but you have to go down to the city dump—now, this very night—and find Shark. I—I'll even go with you, if you'll dig that hole under the fence in my yard big enough for me to squeeze out. After all, I guess this is partly my fault. Once we find Shark, we'll make him an offer he can't refuse. This is what I have in mind. . . ."

Charlie and Jonathan listened to Big Al's plan and slowly nodded their heads. It might work. It just might work.

At least, Jonathan certainly hoped so. Because tomorrow night was the last night the moon would be round—and his very last chance to live the rest of his life as a boy.

CHAPTER TEN

Down in the Dumps

In the eerie light of the silver moon, the city dump seemed like a haunted place. Piles of old tires, broken washing machines, and threadbare sofas loomed on either side of the narrow path, like monsters just waiting to grab the three dogs. Rusted tin cans rolled under their feet, and the darkness was alive with the squeaking, skittering sounds of the rats, mice, and bugs that made their homes in the dump. Somewhere in the distance, there was a steady "bang, bang, bang," as something metal slammed back and forth, back and forth, in the night wind. Jonathan shivered and scooted a little closer to Big Al. It almost sounded like a mad robot, walking the darkness on huge metal feet, searching, searching for a helpless victim. . . .

Cut it out! he told himself. If he ever got out of this mess, he vowed, he would never watch another monster movie on Channel 32.

"Wh-where would this Shark be on a night like this?" he asked, his voice coming out in a frightened whimper. "Wouldn't he be inside where it's warm?"

Charlie snorted. "You don't know Shark," he said. "He's tough, really tough. A little cold and wind aren't going to bother him. Besides—"

"Can it, you two," Big Al interrupted in his softest rumble. "I'm trying to listen for Shark—better that we hear him before he hears us. But with you guys gabbing, he could sneak up on us and we'd all be torn to bits before we even heard him coming."

That didn't make Jonathan feel any better, but he closed his mouth and tiptoed down the path after the big basset hound, tripping over broken toys and greasy fast-food containers as he went. Would Shark bother to chew them up before he swallowed them, he wondered, or would he just gulp them all down whole? What would Mom think when Jonathan never came home again? What would—

"Shh!"

Jonathan tripped over his own paws as Big Al came to a dead stop in the middle of the path just ahead of him. The basset hound's nose lifted, sniffing the wind, and his long, droopy ears twitched with excitement.

"He's around here someplace, guys," Big Al whispered. "Right over there on the other side of that old car, I think. Listen . . . can't you hear him?"

Charlie and Jonathan strained their ears. Sure enough, Jonathan's keen poodle hearing caught the smacking, gnawing, scraping sound of sharp teeth chewing on something hard.

"My chewbone!" he whispered. "That big creep is slobbering all over my chewbone!"

Charlie nudged him with one paw. "Hush," the little white poodle said. "We'll get your chewbone back, don't worry. But you don't know Shark. If you go in there yelling and carrying on about your chewbone, you won't have to worry about spending the rest of your life as a poodle— there won't be that much more of it left to spend."

"So what *are* we supposed to do?" Jonathan demanded crossly. "Call out the Marines? We have to get that bone back!"

"We have a plan, remember?" Big Al reminded him. "It'll work, too—I think. But we have to keep cool heads. We can't just go charging in there growling and snarling, or we'll wind up as Shark's midnight snacks. Now, for the last time, keep quiet and leave it to me, okay?"

"Okay, okay," Jonathan muttered. "But I just hope this works. On top of everything, my fur is getting absolutely filthy!"

The two little poodles took up their positions on either side of Big Al, their pointy black noses twitching with nervousness.

"Slink a little more," the basset hound advised them. "Get your bellies down closer to the ground. That way, Shark will know that *we* know he's the boss. That's the only way he won't mutilate us first thing."

"This is embarrassing," Jonathan grumbled, but he slunk toward the old car with his belly so low it almost brushed the frozen mud.

Big Al stopped just as they reached the back end of the rusty car. From the other side, they could clearly hear the smacking, chewing sounds of Shark as he gnawed on the chewbone. Whatever else you could say about the junkyard dog, he certainly didn't have very good table manners.

The basset hound took a deep breath. Then, "Shark!" he cried in his yodeling howl. "Oh, mighty Shark, master of the city dump, lord of the junkyard! Three of your humble servants wish for a word with you!"

Jonathan stared at Charlie. "Does he have to say all that?" he whispered. "It's downright humiliating!"

"Only if we want to get out of this without having our ears and tails ripped off," the other poodle answered. "Don't worry about it, Jonathan. It doesn't really mean anything. And isn't it worth a little embarrassment to get your chewbone back?"

Behind the car, the chomping, chewing noises came to a sudden halt. There was a moment's silence, so still that Jonathan could almost hear the pounding of his heart. Then, from around the front end of the old car, a dog appeared—the biggest, ugliest, most ferocious-looking dog Jonathan had ever seen. It was all he could do to stand his ground and not run as the huge, dirty-white beast strode toward them, its long, sharp teeth bared in a menacing snarl.

"Yeah?" the dog demanded. "So what makes you think *I* want to talk to *you*? Better beat it, before I turn you all into hamburger."

Jonathan hoped Shark couldn't see the way Big Al was trembling as he answered.

"Hamburger?" the basset hound repeated. "Funny, that's why we came—sort of. We want to talk to you about—about hamburger."

The big white dog lowered his head and fixed a yellow-eyed glare on the basset hound. "What are you talking about?" he demanded. "Let's cut out the games and get to the good part. What do you mean, you want to talk about hamburger?"

"Why, you like hamburger, don't you?" Big Al said, his voice innocent. "Red, juicy,

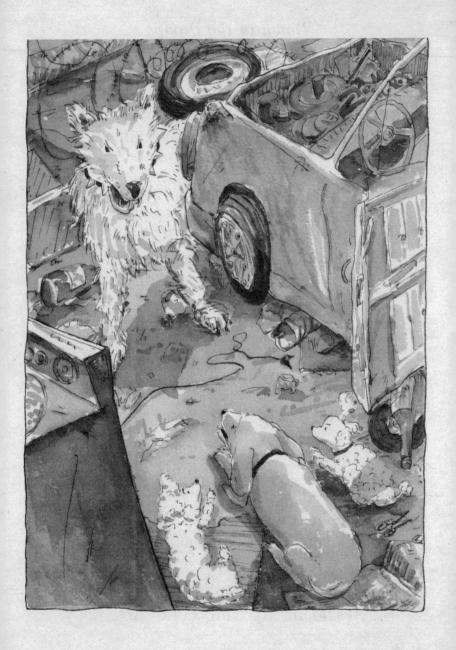

luscious raw hamburger, straight from the supermarket?"

Shark snorted. "So?" he snapped. "What about it?"

"We—we can get you some," Charlie piped up. "Sir," he added nervously, as the big dog swiveled his head to stare at him.

"Yeah?" Shark snarled. "And just why would you want to do that?"

"We—we believe you might have accidentally, uh, borrowed something that belongs to our young friend, here," Big Al answered, nosing Jonathan forward a little. "We thought you might be willing to give the kid a break and trade his chewbone back for a package of hamburger. Five pounds of hamburger, for that one dinky little chewbone. Think about it, Shark. Doesn't sound like a bad offer, does it?"

"Hamburger, huh?" Shark tilted his head, thinking it over. For the first time, Jonathan noticed that the dog's yellow eyes looked glazed and a little stupid. "What's the catch?"

"No catch," Jonathan said hastily, finding his voice. "We just want the chewbone back, that's all."

"Big chewbone?" Shark asked. "Bright green? Kind of funny-tasting?"

Charlie nodded eagerly. "That's the one," he agreed. "If you'll just give it to us, we'll go straight to the supermarket and come back with your hamburger, okay?"

"Not so fast!" Shark frowned. "You think I'm a dummy or something? You don't get your chewbone back till I get my meat. And that's another thing. I don't want any cheap old hamburger. I want a steak. A thick, juicy, chewy steak—the biggest one they've got. Bring back some dinky little dried-up thing, and the deal's off. Got it?"

"That—that's fine," Big Al said, nodding very fast. "You'll have your steak, Shark. The only thing is, it's getting late. The supermarket will probably be closed by the time we could get there. Would tomorrow night be okay? We'll meet you here, oh say two hours after moonrise. You have the chewbone, and we'll have your steak."

The big white dog grinned, showing dozens of knife-sharp teeth. "You better," he growled. "Try any funny stuff, and *you'll* be the raw meat."

"Yes, sir," Big Al gulped. "Of course, sir. We wouldn't think of cheating you, sir."

"You're boring me," Shark snarled. "I don't like dogs who bore me. Now *get!*"

He took only one step toward them, but that was enough. All three dogs yelped, whirled, and flew back down the narrow path, hardly noticing the sharp rocks and shards of glass that cut their tender paw pads. They didn't stop until they were through the junkyard gate and out on the road again. There they paused, panting, to catch their breath.

"Tomorrow night?" Jonathan complained as soon as he could speak. "That's cutting things a little close, isn't it?"

"Can't be helped," Big Al answered. "The stores are all closed by now. We have to wait till they open again—unless you have a big, juicy steak at home in your freezer, that is. Then it will be easy."

Jonathan shook his head. "Are you kidding?" he asked. "On my mom's salary? We're lucky to get hamburger! Exactly where do you expect me to come up with this steak you promised that monster?"

"Use your allowance and buy one tomorrow after school," Charlie suggested. "That should be simple enough."

"Simple for you, maybe," Jonathan grumbled. "I've spent all last month's allowance, and I don't get this month's until Mom's payday, three days from now. By then, it will be too late!"

Charlie sighed. "Then we'll have to do it the hard way," he said. "We'll have to sneak into the supermarket tomorrow night and take a steak."

"But—but that's stealing!" Jonathan protested. "We can't do that!"

"It isn't stealing if you go in and pay for it as soon as you get your allowance," Big

Al suggested. "You could tell them your dog took some meat, and you're paying them back. That would be the truth, too—well, sort of, anyway."

Jonathan thought about it. "I guess I could do that," he agreed. "I'm pretty desperate. But how are we supposed to get into the store to take the meat? They don't let dogs inside supermarkets, unless they're Seeing Eye dogs."

"I know just how we can do it," Charlie said. "Leave it all to me. You two meet me at the back door of the market, in the alley, just as soon as Jonathan gets finished changing into his poodle shape. Don't worry, Jonathan. This time tomorrow night, your troubles will all be over."

"Yeah," Jonathan agreed, "once Shark rips me into a million tiny pieces, I won't have anything at all to worry about, ever again."

All three dogs were very quiet as they wearily padded their way toward home.

CHAPTER ELEVEN

One T-Bone, Extra-Rare

"Where have you guys been?" Jonathan yipped as his friends trotted up the alley behind the supermarket. "I've been waiting here for almost an hour!"

Charlie darted an uneasy look over his shoulder at the alley. "We had a little trouble," he explained. "Big Al here didn't show up when I thought he would, so I got uneasy and went to check on him. He hadn't even left his yard yet!"

"It wasn't my fault," Big Al explained.

"Vince saw the hole Charlie dug under the fence last night, and he filled it in this afternoon. I'm not a very good digger, and I couldn't dig my way out."

"So I had to dig a new hole," Charlie went on. "The problem was, Vince came out and caught me digging, just when the hole was large enough for Big Al to start wiggling through. He tried to grab Big Al, so I—so I . . ." He stopped, shaking his head.

"So he bit Vince," the basset hound finished. His long, wrinkled face looked even more mournful than usual. "I'm really in for it when I get home. I've never seen the kid so mad. I'll be lucky if he doesn't chain me up for a month."

"I'm sorry you got in trouble because of me," Jonathan said. "But let's worry about it later, okay? The supermarket will be closing in an hour, and we still have to get that steak. If I don't get the chewbone back tonight, I could wind up in the pound!"

"Calm down," Charlie answered. "We

can do it. All we have to do is hide behind these garbage cans and wait until a delivery truck comes. The bakery usually brings a whole truckload of bread and cookies sometime during the evening."

As quietly as they could, the three dogs squeezed behind the row of garbage cans. They didn't have long to wait. It wasn't even ten minutes before the big white bakery van rumbled its way down the alley, stopping at the back door of the market.

"This is our chance, guys," Charlie said. "Wait until he's got a big tray full of bread. Then sneak in right behind him, and don't let him see you, whatever you do."

That part of their plan went without a hitch. Loaded down with bread, rolls, and hamburger buns, the deliveryman didn't even notice the three dogs who sneaked silently in at his heels, past the huge swinging door and into the dimly lit storeroom at the back of the market.

Still silently, the dogs quickly found hiding places—Big Al behind a cardboard box filled with paper towels, Charlie and Jonathan behind a stack of detergent boxes. The deliveryman pushed through another door with his tray full of bread, and the three dogs waited impatiently for a few minutes, until the man appeared again, whistling as he hurried back through the alley door to his waiting van.

"Now!" Charlie whispered and they came out of their hiding places, their toe-nails clicking on the concrete floor. "Big Al," Charlie went on, "you're too big to go into the store—someone would notice you first thing. You stay out here and be ready to jump in if we get into trouble. We'll signal by barking. If you hear us, don't waste a minute coming to our help."

"Got it," said the basset hound, his face solemn.

"The meat counter is at the side of the store," Jonathan reminded Charlie. "We'll have to sneak through quite a bit of market before we get to the meat."

"That will be the tricky part," Charlie

agreed. "We'll just have to do our best to stay out of sight. And if someone spots you—well, just don't get caught, whatever you do. The pound is the last place I want to end up."

"Let's just do it," Jonathan said. "All this talking is making me nervous."

The door into the supermarket was too heavy for the little poodles to budge alone, but with all three dogs pushing, they managed to open it.

"Good luck," Big Al whispered as the others slipped through.

The two little dogs stood still for a moment, blinking in the sudden bright light of the store. All around them rose the wonderful smells of a thousand delicious things to eat—hot dogs and potato chips, chocolate cookies and chewy caramels, steaks and roasts and chicken wings. But they didn't have time to enjoy the mouthwatering aromas.

"Quick!" Charlie whispered. "Which way is the meat counter?"

"Over here," Jonathan answered, trotting to his right. "Head for that display of cornflakes. We should be safe there for a second."

Scuttling behind the stack of cereal boxes, the two poodles stuck cautious heads out for a look around.

"I don't see anyone," Jonathan began. "I think we can go now—no, wait! Here comes a shopping cart!"

Pulling their heads back in, they waited until a little old lady had tottered past, dropping a box of cornflakes into her cart. Then, slowly, carefully, they sneaked from behind the cereal.

"Over there!" said Charlie. "Behind the row of potted plants!"

In the florist section of the store, the white poodles blended in almost invisibly behind the pots of white chrysanthemums, although the strong, spicy odors of the flowers nearly made Jonathan sneeze. They waited there while a teenage boy selected a long-stemmed red rose for his giggling girlfriend. Then, as soon as the coast was clear, they shot out from behind the flowers and dashed to their next hiding place, under a table loaded with day-old powdered doughnuts.

Slowly, they worked their way across the supermarket, darting from hiding place to hiding place—behind a rack of magazines, under a shelf of canned soup, between two freezer cases filled with ice cream and frozen vegetables. As they went, they had to dodge young mothers filling their carts with baby food, women reading greeting cards, men choosing frozen dinners. But, although they had one or two close calls, luck was with them—no one seemed to see the two little white poodles.

"We're almost there now," Jonathan whispered, as they dashed around a display of paperback books. "The meat counter is just one aisle away. Once we get there, we have to—"

"Oh, no!" Charlie gasped. "Look, here

comes one of the store people! Quick, where can we hide?"

They glanced frantically everywhere, but there didn't seem to be any hiding place close enough. They were in the middle of a wide, open aisle, and the stock boy was coming closer and closer with his cart full of stuffed animals for the toy display.

"The toys!" Jonathan breathed. "Quick!"

Just in the nick of time, the two poodles reached the low shelf of stuffed animals. They pushed their way through the teddy bears and fuzzy lions and tigers, then plopped down on the shelf among the animals and froze, not even daring to breathe. Only their bright black eyes gave them away as they sat there, perfectly still, trying their hardest to look like stuffed poodles.

In spite of himself, Jonathan had to fight the urge to bark and run as the stock boy began to unload his cart and arrange stuffed animals all around them. A fuzzy plush zebra plopped down beside him, and a big furry black cat landed right in front of him, its fluffy tail brushing across his nose and almost making him sneeze.

It seemed like a hundred years before the stock boy finished arranging the animals and headed back down the aisle, pushing his empty cart. Then they had to wait while two women strolled by, arguing about the price of pork roast. Finally, the coast was clear, and the two little dogs stepped down from the toy shelf on shaky legs.

"That was a close one!" Charlie said. "Quick thinking, Jonathan. Now let's get that steak!"

A minute later, they arrived at the meat section. Just as Jonathan had remembered, there was a little table at the end of the meat counter, filled with bottles of steak sauce and packages of meat tenderizer.

"Up you go!" Charlie urged him as he struggled to jump onto the table.

After a few tries, he made it, pulling

himself up by his front legs. From there it was an easy jump into the meat compartment. Jonathan shivered as the cold air of the refrigerated case swirled around his legs. But he didn't have time to worry about that. Running as fast as he could down the very middle of the pot roasts, chickens, and sausages, he headed for the steaks at the end of the meat case.

He had just grabbed a big, thick, juicy T-bone, biting down hard through the plastic tray and wrap, when he heard a scream.

"Eeeeek!"

Jonathan looked up to see a woman in a pants suit, pointing straight at him.

"Eeeeek! There's a dog in the meat case! Someone come quick, there's a dog in the meat case!"

"I'm out of here," Jonathan mumbled around a mouthful of plastic.

Holding onto the T-bone for dear life, he climbed to the edge of the meat case and launched himself out into the air, hitting

the floor with a thud. A second later a yipping Charlie joined him, and the two poodles scrambled for the storeroom door, with a parade of stock boys and checkout clerks running after them, screaming and shaking their fists.

Big Al was waiting at the door. He had heard Charlie's frantic barks and had the door open and waiting for them. A second later, they were in the cool, dark storeroom. Then Big Al ran full-tilt across the room and hit the outside door with his shoulder. The door flew open, and they all piled outside, tumbling over each other in the darkness of the alley.

"Run!" Charlie shouted breathlessly. "They're right behind us!"

So they ran, Jonathan still holding onto the steak, until the sound of their pursuers faded behind them. They stopped in front of a little white house on the corner of Sycamore and Walnut, their breath coming in little, panting gasps.

"We made it!" Big Al said jubilantly.

"We made it! Your troubles are over, Jonathan!"

"Not quite," he reminded him. "We still have to get that chewbone from Shark. What if he's changed his mind? What if he won't give it to us?"

"You don't have to worry about that," Charlie assured him. "A dog's word is always good, even if the dog is a monster like Shark. Besides, can you see him passing up that gorgeous steak? I don't think so!"

Fifteen minutes later, a drooling Shark snatched the T-bone steak from Jonathan's teeth, ripping right through the plastic wrap in his hurry to get at the juicy meat.

"But what about my chewbone?" Jonathan yelped.

"Oh, yeah. That." Shark jerked his head toward an old sewing machine in the shadows. "It's under that. Take it and get lost."

The chewbone was so big and heavy that Big Al had to carry it as they rushed through the gates of the dump. Then they were off down the muddy road, pelting toward Mr. Bruce's house as fast as they could go.

The round moon cast eerie shadows as they ran. Hurry, their scampering paws seemed to say. Hurry, hurry, hurry . . .

CHAPTER TWELVE

Wolfbane
with Ketchup

Jonathan looked at the big green chew-bone lying on Mr. Bruce's kitchen floor. He was almost afraid to take the first nibble. What if it didn't work?

"Go ahead," Mr. Bruce urged him softly. "You don't have much time, Jonathan. Take a bite."

Jonathan sniffed at the big, soft bathrobe that Mr. Bruce had draped around him. If the chewbone worked, he'd be needing that robe soon. If not . . . Jonathan couldn't stand to think about it.

"Don't just nibble," Charlie advised him. "Bite down hard. Give it a good chew."

Nervously, Jonathan nipped at the chewbone. Then he made a face.

"Maybe it's just because I haven't been a dog very long," he said, "but I don't know what Shark saw in this thing. It tastes awfully funny to me."

Mr. Bruce had been watching him closely. He seemed to know right away what the problem was.

"Here," he said, stumping across the room with a bottle of ketchup. Bending over, he doused the chewbone with the thick red stuff. "Maybe this will help."

"Well, it couldn't make it any *worse*," Jonathan said in a doggy grumble. "Here I go again."

The ketchup didn't do much to disguise the strange taste of the wolfbane, but it helped just enough for Jonathan to take a big bite, then another.

"Jonathan!" Charlie breathed. "I—I think it's working! I see patches of skin through your fur!"

Jonathan looked down at himself. Sure enough, there were pink places showing through all that white hair. He looked at Charlie's excited face. Then he looked at Big Al, who was waiting anxiously beside Mr. Bruce's chair.

"Then I may not be able to understand you two again," he suddenly realized. "Charlie, Big Al, I—I just want to thank you. You really are friends."

"Think nothing of it," Big Al rumbled, while Charlie nodded. "We're glad it's working out for you. Now hurry—get the job done!"

Jonathan made a face as he took another nibble of the chewbone. He could feel himself getting bigger, bigger, bigger. As he took a final bite, he felt the last of the white fur melting from his arms, his shoulders, his face. And then—and then . . .

"Jonathan!" It was Mr. Bruce's excited voice. "You're back again! It really is you!"

Looking down at his bare legs and feet, Jonathan saw that it was true. He was a boy again—a real, live, human boy. Turning red, he belted the sash of the robe around his middle.

"How can I thank you?" he said. "How can I thank all of you?"

"By getting home to your mother before she gets worried about you," Mr. Bruce answered, while Charlie and Big Al sniffed excitedly about Jonathan's ankles. "You don't want her to find out you sneaked out tonight, do you? Oh, and boy, if I were you, I'd climb in through your bedroom window and put some clothes on before she sees you. You could give her a terrible shock!"

Silently as a shadow, Jonathan let himself out of Mr. Bruce's yard and headed down the sidewalk toward his own house, the two dogs trotting at his heels. He was halfway home when a sudden sound made him freeze. Click, click, click—what was that, hurrying toward them in the darkness?

Charlie whined, and Big Al's growl vibrated in his throat.

"What is it?" Jonathan asked. "Who's

there? Oh, I wish you guys could still talk to me!"

Then, into the pool of light cast by the streetlight, came something covered with gray curly fur, something with a panting pink tongue. Even before Big Al yelped wildly and trotted toward the new dog, Jonathan knew.

"Vince!" he gasped, sinking down to the curb. "Vince, it's you, isn't it?" He looked down at Charlie. "It must have happened when you bit him tonight," he said. "You've done it again, Charlie!"

All three of the dogs wagged frantic tails at him.

"You'd better follow Charlie to Mr. Bruce's house," Jonathan told the poodle. "He has the chewbone. And you'd better hurry, Vince—it will be moonset before long."

The three dogs trotted through the gate and up the sidewalk toward the wizard's front door.

For a moment Jonathan stared after

them, remembering what it felt like to run wild in the night. Then, tightening the belt of the rumpled robe, he headed for his bedroom window.

The tarnished silver moon was just sliding behind the trees as he hoisted himself onto the window ledge. He sat there for a moment, staring out into the night. From somewhere far away, a dog's eerie howl floated through the darkness, and the sound brought goose bumps to Jonathan's arms. Quickly, he threw his legs over the windowsill and dropped to the floor.

It was good to be home.